Sing a Song of Sixpence

Copyright © 1976 by Mary Tozer
First published in Great Britain 1976 by
World's Work Ltd
The Windmill Press
Kingswood Tadworth Surrey

Printed in Great Britain by
William Clowes & Sons Limited,
London, Beccles and Colchester

SBN 437 79417 2

Sing a Song of Sixpence

A World's Work Children's Book

Sing a song of sixpence a pocket full of rye

Four and twenty blackbirds

Baked in a pie

When the pie was opened

The birds began to sing

Was not that a dainty dish to set before the king?

The king was in the counting-house

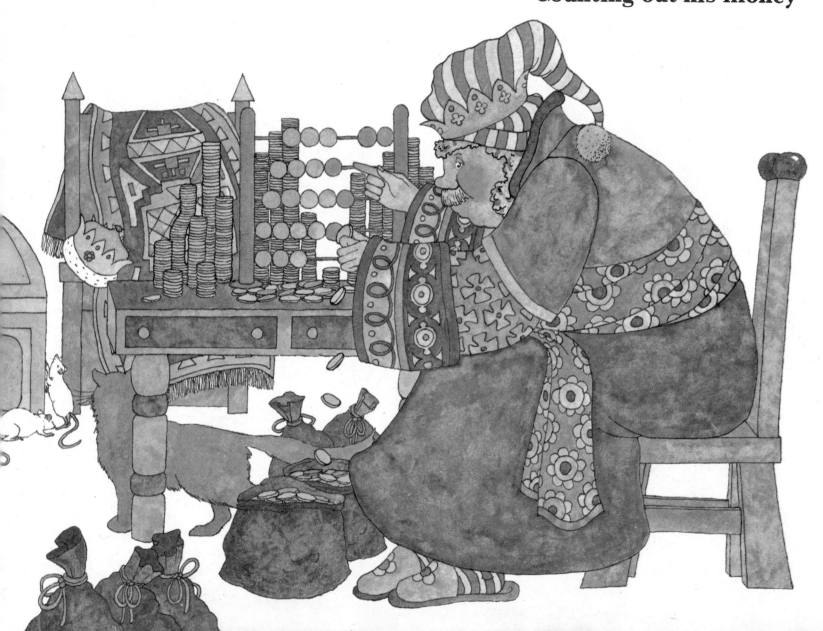

Counting out his money

The queen was in the parlour
eating bread and honey

The maid was in the garden hanging out the clothes

When down came a blackbird and pecked off her nose.

They sent for the king's doctor

Who sewed it on again

And he sewed it on so neatly,

the seam was never seen.